HAUNTED TACOS

HAUNTED TACOS

Culinary Verse With a Curse

Written and illustrated by
Shannon Keegan

SCHOLASTIC INC.
New York Toronto London Auckland Sydney

ISBN 0-590-45815-9

12 11 10 9 8 7 6 5 4 3 2 1   2 3 4 5 6 7/9

Printed in the U.S.A.   23

First Scholastic printing, September 1992

For Dylan and Lauren,
my favorite monsters

Contents

DUNGEON DINING

Darkness rules the atmosphere
   at our dungeon restaurant.
And if gruesome food is what you need,
   then we've got what you want.

There's spider mousse and bat hors d'oeuvres
   with a relish made of lizards,
Weasel snouts and aardvark toes
   and earlobe minced with gizzards.

A bowl of eyes, a plate of lips —
   the hairy soup is fine.
A salad full of beetle wings
   makes a dinner date divine!

And what about desserts, my friend?
   Your weight is rather wanting.
We've bones enough for soups and stews,
   for sauces, roasts, and hauntings.

So, eat up there! And chow right down
   'til your bloated belly's fed.
And if you cannot pay the bill,
   we'll simply shrink your head.

9

MORLOCK'S ONE-HEADED, TWO-HEADED STEW

Chef Morlock makes a monster-ous stew,
  he cooks it to a grimy goo
  and serves it hot for me and you,
Chef Morlock's one-headed, two-headed stew.

The ingredients are unusually few:
  he adds some toes — just a few —
  a hairy chin, an arm (with tattoo)
All par for course in Morlock's stew.

Discussing the gruel with you-know-who,
  I was told that knees were unpleasant to chew
  and that hands were especially hard to subdue,
So they're banned from the one-headed, two-headed stew.

But a problem exists with this bloody brew,
  I see but one head that floats into view
  (though the Chef would be thrilled to put yours in
  there, too),
Chef Morlock's one-headed, two-headed stew.

10

THE LOATHSOME LUNCHEON

My rabid rats have run away,
My roaches left the table,
But Horace brought them back to me
With cream cheese on a bagel.

Wicked William threw his shoe,
It landed in a custard.
It startled my dear python so,
And my Gila monster's flustered.

Naughty Boris caught a fly
And wouldn't even share it.
So I put a stinkbug in his hat
And encouraged him to wear it.

I can't imagine dining out
With a normal kind of feller.
And if one came to call on me,
I'd lock him in the cellar!

LOUELLA'S COFFIN TIPS

Louella Prune
Howls at the moon
And lectures on
Manners and etiquette:

"Don't be caught dead
Eating in bed
Like my cousins
In Northern Connecticut.

"Ever so often,
Tidy your coffin
And clean up the food
That you hide in it.

"Or one summer's day
The neighbors might say
That something or someone
Surely died in it!"

HAUNTED TACOS

Haunted tacos,
Pudding and pie.
Bite the bats
And make them fly!
When the bats come out to play,
Haunted tacos
Fly away!

DAVEY'S MONSTER CAFE

In the chilliest, dankest part of the town
There's a place where the old ghoulies gather.
Slithering, creeping, and groping around,
They bellow, burp, slobber, and blather.

I'm talking about Davey's Monster Cafe
Where the beetle-blood burgers are better.
Where the blood-sucking zombie queen goes for buffet
And eats all she wants — 'cos they let her.

The mummies are dining and so are the dads,
The vampires soon will be winging it.
And through the dark night, a dirge from the lads
Echoes near, and here's how they're singing it:

Special
Bat Soup

"Tuna tongues, badger lungs, cobwebs and cake —
Bring me some bones and some muscles.
Dig up worms and a heart with a stake,
Then fetch me my red-blood corpuscles.

"I'm the worst kind of monster that you'll ever see
'Cos I'm terribly, horribly rude:
My manners are nil and forget them I will
If you come between me and my food!"

DEADMAN DINNER

My eye fell out and landed "plunk!"
Into my vichyssoise it sunk.
I'm startled at these bits of face
Falling off around my place.
My nose was running (and never came back)
My teeth are brown, my jaw quite slack.
When both my ears fell off my head,
I figured out I must be dead.

TOADWICH

I ate a toad to make a point —
Chomped everything above the joint:
Feeties, nose, and eyes and belly,
Ate it all on toast with jelly.

Shocked my granny and my mum
When I asked, would they like some?
"Oh, heavens no!" my granny squirms,
"Your mum and I prefer earthworms!"

MABEL'S MIDNIGHT SNACK

"Thump!" The onion bumped and rolled across the table.
The eerie light of midnight
    swirled around the hands of Mabel.

With a swipe and a "plopppff!" she drenched the bread
    with mayonnaise.
Then the mustard, cheese, and pickled beets
    were applied in frightening ways.

Soon a wretched moan arose from that strange sandwich
    Mabel wanted,
And as she sunk her teeth into the crust —
    too late! The snack was haunted!!

With skin turned white, and eyes rolled up into her
    shaking head,
Her teeth grew long like the fangs of a dog;
    one might think she'd soon be dead.

Then she vanished in a puff of smoke — or what? Tell us
    if you're able
What became of that odd sandwich
    and our ghostly, hungry Mabel?

GARLIC BLUES

Most vampires I have known
Consider threats just useless drivel,
But garlic makes the beasties run
Or, like prunes, they tend to shrivel.

With a vampire you could argue lots —
Over stakes and crosses quibble,
But to keep them from your dining room,
Serve the stuff they'd *never* nibble:

Garlic toast and garlic bagels,
Garlic roasted, stewed, and stuffed,
Garlic tea and garlic cookies —
Garlic cake that's garlic-truffled!

And when you summon all your dinner guests
Those vampires won't participate.
It's not the soup or cheese you chose,
It's that garlic stuff you know they hate.

ODE TO MOLD

Mold,
So I'm told
Is best served
When cold.

Or instead,
When it's dead,
On a piece of
French bread.

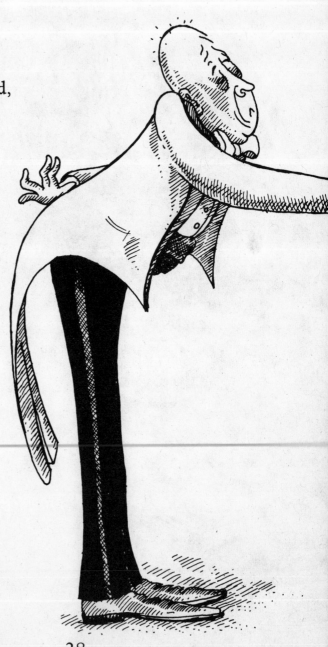

NEWT SONG

A newt in your boot
　will make you scoot.
　　Will make you choke
　　　on your toast and fruit!
　　　And hoot
　　　　and shoot
　　　a hole in your suit
　　whilst in pursuit
of the tiny brute
　who calls himself
　　a newt.

HIDE AND SHRIEK

I wonder where that arachnid hid?
   Under the lid
   Of the pot from Madrid?
   I'll bet he did.

Through a place too small for most he slid,
And came to a halt with a spidery skid.
   Under the lid
   Of the pot from Madrid?
   I'll bet he did.

HE DID!!!

FRANK DINES OUT

Bolts in the neck are a drag.
For they cause the spaghetti to snag.
  It tickles like heck
  All hung up in his neck
And it threatens to make Frankie ga-ga-gag,
It threatens to make Frankie gag.

Ingesting a hunk of fresh liver
Is enough to make *this* monster shiver.
  His esophagus freezes,
  His trachea wheezes,
And his stomachs, all three, start to qui-qui-quiver,
His stomachs and knees start to quiver.

BUGGIE STEW

16 shiny centipedes,
      rentipedes,
      tentipedes,
16 fancy centipedes
Were dancing in a row.

20 mashed potato bugs,
      dato bugs,
      bato bugs,
20 squished potato bugs
Were humming rather low.

Jumped they did into a pot,
      pinto a pot,
      winto a pot,
Jumped they did into a pot
To the soupy down below.

Now 36 yummy bugs,
      tummy bugs,
      funny bugs,
Now 36 squirmy bugs
Star in the dinner show.

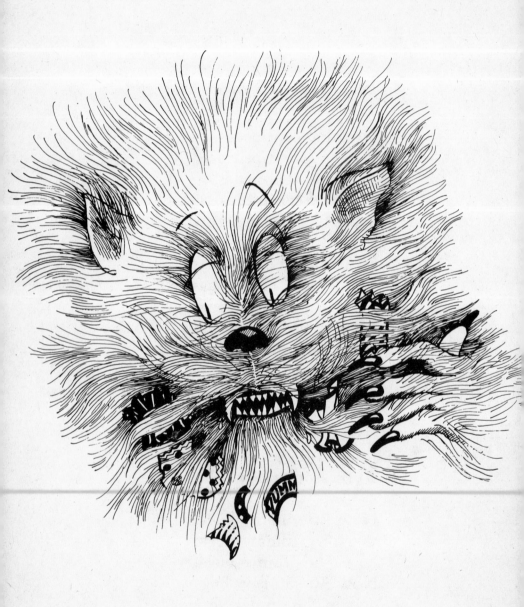

THE WEREWOLF SLOB

I fear the werewolf is a slob.
I heard this from my cousin Bob:
   He eats a lot of candy when
     he's feeling rather weird and then
   He tucks wrappers
     in his beard and when
   It's breezy
     the beard gets cleared again —
       except for that marshmallow jelly-bean glob,
Which is why the werewolf is a slob.

Look for other scary stories
you might enjoy:

———————————

Rattle Your Bones: Skeleton Drawing Fun
David Clemesha and Andrea Griffing Zimmerman

•

Never Say Boo to a Ghost
John Foster and Korky Paul

•

The Spookiest Day
David Gantz

•

101 Bug Jokes
Lisa Eisenberg and Katy Hall